STAT

SLAM DUNK

by *AMAR'E STOUDEMIRE*
illustrated by *TIM JESSELL*

SCHOLASTIC PRESS / NEW YORK

To the children of the world. I hope you all find the success and peace that comes from reading and learning.

*   *   *

Special thanks to Michael Northrop

ISBN 978-0-545-48876-1

Cover and interior art by Tim Jessell
Original cover design by Yaffa Jaskoll

12 11 10 9 8 7 6 5 4 3 2 1   13 14 15 16 17 18/0

Printed in the U.S.A.   23

First printing, January 2013

I climbed down out of the front seat of my dad's old truck and slammed the door behind me. My face was hot even before the heat blazed up from the sun-baked parking lot. I'd been invited to another basketball tournament. But instead of thinking about the first practice that was about to start, I was angry because Dad and I had had a dumb argument on the ride over.

Shake it off, Amar'e, I told myself. Before I even looked up, the sound of rims rattling, balls bouncing, and kids hollering told me where I needed to go. My first good look at the court told me what I already knew: These kids were good. I saw silky crossover dribbles and shots dropping in as smooth as rainwater. And they were older, too. I'd already been told I was the youngest kid they'd invited, and now I could see it. I felt my stomach tighten a little with nerves.

Dad's run-down truck somehow managed to drive off, slowly. The engine revved, the wheels turned, and the truck backfired loudly as it pulled away. It was sounding bad lately. On the ride over I'd made the mistake of asking him when he was going to get it fixed. Man, that did it: *When am I supposed to find the time for that?* he'd snapped.

Dad always had busy times and quiet times at work. I think that's just part of running a lawn-care company. But this busy time had gone on and on. I usually helped out on the weekends, but now I had practice instead. The last thing Dad had said before I got out: *Got to go pick up the extra guy.*

Dad made his point — he wouldn't need an extra guy if I helped out — and I made mine when I slammed the door. Didn't he understand that this was my biggest tourney yet? It was an opportunity to really step up my game. Wasn't that more important than pushing a lawn mower for the millionth time?

Everyone on the court turned to look at me after the truck backfired. I was really starting things off with a bang. They sized me up as I headed toward them. I didn't understand why they kept looking my way until a guy came up behind me and startled me.

"You Amar'e?" he said.

"Yeah."

"Yes, *Coach*," he said.

Well, at least I knew who he was now.

"Yes, Coach," I said.

"Well, report to the court."

The way the guy moved and talked made me feel like I'd accidentally signed up for the army instead of the tourney. He was dressed that way, too, with a short-sleeve shirt tucked into khaki pants that were way too heavy for the Florida weather. His head wasn't shaved, but it might as well have been: The hair was buzz-cut down to about four millimeters. He pulled some keys out of his pocket and headed over to a big red car.

My friend Jammer met me at the edge of the court. His full name was James Jamison, but I'd only heard anyone say it once. He was coming over to say hi, but also to sort of vouch for me — to let the others know he knew me and that I was okay. Jammer was an amazing player, and I appreciated it.

"A-ten-hut! I'm here to report to the court," I said.

He smiled: "You sound like Coach Commando over there."

"Is that really his name?" I said with a laugh.

"Nah, it's Dunn. He's a little *over*-Dunn sometimes, but he's not so bad."

"As long as you hit your shots," said a familiar voice.

"Hey, Khalid," I said.

He was another guy I knew from the last tournament. Khalid was short and it looked like someone had inflated him with a bicycle pump. I don't mean that in a bad way. He wasn't fat, but he was kind of . . . thick, I guess. I think the word is *stocky*.

But somehow he was still as fast as a sprinter and as agile as an acrobat. Not only was he a point guard, he was the best one I'd ever played with. I guess it helped that he had the permanent element of surprise. No matter how many times I saw that cobra-strike quick first step come from those thick legs of his, I still couldn't believe it. Anyway, he was a good guy: funny, confident, and friendly.

I looked around. *I may only know two guys here*, I thought, *but they're good ones.* And then Coach Dunn came back from his car, and things got serious as he began barking out his orders.

CHAPTER 2

*T*here was no need to split up into teams — they'd already done that before I arrived in Dad's hunk of junk. Coach just stuck me with the guys who were down a player and got things started. Jammer was on my team, but Khalid was on the other side. I looked around at the others, and it really sunk in how big they were. It's not that they were that much taller than me. I was pretty tall — not just tall for my age, but tall for a human. I was already taller than most of my teachers.

But these guys were starting to fill out and add real muscle. I felt like a sixth grader wandering into an eighth-grade gym class, which is actually what I was kind of doing. Except instead of phys ed, these were the best ballers their age. Before I could think anything more, I had the basketball in my hands. The first practice game was underway, and my team had won the tip. The guy D'ing me was named Wayne. He wasn't on me all that tight, so I dribbled it a few times as we headed up the court.

At least the ball hadn't grown any. It felt familiar in my hand, and I started to settle down. The ball was the same size, the court was the same size, and the basket was definitely the same size. And I was good at this. I may not have been as big or as old as most of these guys, but I hadn't just wandered in here off the highway. I was invited to play in this tourney, same as them.

A guard from the other team tried to sneak up behind me for the steal. I executed a quick crossover and left him swatting at air. But that reminded me: I wasn't the guy who was supposed to be bringing the ball all the way up the court. I was usually a power forward, but I was basically a swing on this team. That's like a mix of small forward and shooting guard.

I looked for our point guard, a kid named Daniel. We made eye contact. He flicked his eyes to the left. It was a tiny move, but I caught it. He was telling me which way he was going. He burst into the open with impressive speed as I launched a pass, leading him just enough.

He plucked the ball from the air and started dribbling. He got down low so that no one could steal it. But the main thing was the way he dribbled. It was a point guard dribble, like Khalid's: totally comfortable, never looking down, like he was born with a basketball in his hand. I knew our offense was in good hands, so I sprinted over to get position near the hoop.

By the time I did, the possession was already over. Daniel found Jammer cutting to the rim. Anyone who was wondering where he got that nickname just found out. He rose up like a rocket and threw down a rim-rattling, one-handed jam.

"Come on, Braylon, put a body on that little dude," a low voice rumbled.

In what world was Jammer a "little dude"? I wondered, as I turned to see who'd said it.

"My bad, Monster," said the guy who was supposed to be defending Jammer.

In Monster's world, I realized, everyone was a little

dude. A lot of the kids were starting to fill out, but this one straight up looked like a man already. And not a nice man, either. Not only did he have muscles, his muscles had muscles.

He saw me sizing him up and shot me a nasty look. It wasn't mean as much as dismissive, like I was nothing. I ignored him and headed the other way on defense. I don't know if he planned it or not, but after a few quick switches on D, I found myself guarding Monster. It felt like standing in traffic.

We were still up near the top of the key, pretty far from the basket. He turned and started backing me down anyway.

Oof! He bumped into me. I tried to shuffle my feet, lean in, not give too much ground.

OOF! He bumped into me again, harder this time. I reached out and swatted at the ball. His dribble was high and off to the side, and I thought I might be able to knock the ball free. I didn't.

OOF! I looked over at Coach Dunn. He didn't even have a whistle, much less any urge to use it. I'm not sure if Monster could've backed me all the way into the basket before I got a hand on the ball or had to climb on his back to get a foul. I'm glad I didn't have to find out. Jammer saw what was going on and jumped in to double-team him.

With two pairs of hands swatting at the ball, Monster had to give it up. When he did, our defense reset. Our center, Tevin, hadn't missed any meals himself. He switched back onto Monster. Jammer went back to guarding Braylon, and I switched back onto Wayne. And tried to catch my breath.

We were all getting a little worn down by the heat, and I switched onto a guy whose dribble was high and lazy to begin with. I went for the steal, slapping out with my hand as I darted forward.

I felt the slap of leather against my palm. When I looked up, the only thing between me and the basket at the other end was the ball, bouncing just ahead of me. I was off and running before anyone else knew what was happening. I had such a clear path to the basket that the only person who ran hard after me was the guy whose pocket I'd picked.

I reached top speed by midcourt. By the time I got to

the foul line I was thinking about what I wanted to do with the ball: lay it up off the backboard or maybe finger-roll it straight into the hoop. But the one thing I *really* wanted to do, I couldn't.

Believe me, I'd tried to dunk the ball. I'd tried it almost every practice. Most of the time, it was just like this, streaking down the court at top speed. If wishing hard made you jump higher, I'd be jamming it by now. But wishing hard just made it hurt more when you doinked it off the rim. And that's what I did when I tried to dunk, unless I lost control on the way up. I was close, but you know how many points you get for close? Zero.

I reached the hoop and laid it up and in.

The players behind me erupted into a chorus of hoots and hollers and laughs. They were waiting for the dunk, too. I turned in time to see the guy I'd stolen the ball from imitating my layup. He raised his front knee high and extended his right hand into the air, palm up. He exaggerated it and put a goofy, tongue-out look on his face.

He'd turned the ball over, but somehow I was the one burning with embarrassment. As I headed back on

defense, I heard them all around me. They were talking about what they would've done if they'd had the ball: dunk it two-handed or throw it down with one.

Right then, Khalid took off at top speed with the ball, and everyone had to take off with him. Khalid was on the other team, but I honestly think he did that for me, just to shut everyone up. The last thing I heard as I put my head down and started running was: "Nice layup, Pee-wee."

From the low rumble of the voice, I knew it was Monster. But I didn't look at him. I didn't want him to see how much it was bothering me. I was as tall as a lot of these guys, and I definitely worked just as hard: Why couldn't I dunk yet? And why did they all have to know?

CHAPTER 3

*T*he ride home was pretty bad. Dad was tired, I was tired, and the truck was exhausted.

"Wash up for dinner," Dad said as we pulled into the driveway.

Normally I'd help him unload the truck, but he didn't ask and as grouchy as he was, I wasn't going to volunteer. I went inside and washed up with Dad's heavy-duty work soap. By the time I was done, my older brother, Junior, was home.

"Something smells good," I said.

Junior held up a big bag from the local supermarket. Dinner! In addition to all the rows of soda, cereal, and frozen food, the supermarket had a section near the meat counter where they sold hot food, right down to the mashed potatoes and side dishes. It looked like my bro had cleaned them out, and it was a good thing, too. As tired as Dad and I had been on the ride home, that was how hungry we were now. And Junior, well, he could always put it back.

We said a quick prayer and then got down to business. I looked around the table as we ate. My dad and brother were big, strong dudes. And my brother was a fierce basketball player himself. No one would ever call either of them Pee-wee. I put another forkful of garlic mashed potatoes in my mouth. *Maybe this will be the mouthful that gets me up and over the rim,* I thought. Well, that and: *Mmmmmm!*

After a while, our eating slowed down to a normal level.

"You over at that new job today, the one on the other side of the lake?" Junior asked Dad.

"Yep," said Dad. "First day."

"So how'd it go?"

"Not so great," said Dad. At first, it seemed like that was all he was going to say on the matter. Then he started talking. Once he did, you could see he was glad to be able to unload a little. There were two main problems. The guy who hired him was being a pain. And the new guy didn't seem to know which end of a mower was which.

"I told this fella to watch out for the gravel," said Dad.

"He didn't . . . ," said Junior.

"Yep, passed right over it with the push mower, sprayed gravel everywhere," said Dad. "Lucky he didn't break any windows or chew up that mower."

I winced when I heard that part. The push mower was usually my job. It's not like I was the world's best grass trimmer, but I definitely knew enough not to try to mow rocks!

Dad didn't say anything to me. He didn't even look my way. In a way, that was worse.

There was a knock on the door after dinner. "I'll get it!" I yelled. Not that I needed to. The other two didn't so much as look up. We all knew it was for me. I went to the kitchen and opened the door.

"Yeah, what do you want?" I said.

"A friend who doesn't keep us waiting at the door for five minutes," said Deuce.

"Yeah, maybe one who's a little cooler, too," said Mike.

I rolled my eyes and stepped aside, and they strolled into the kitchen like they owned the place. Mike and Deuce were my best friends, and they'd been coming over for years. Sometimes, like tonight, they'd just stop by.

"How was practice?" Mike asked me.

I just shrugged.

"That bad, huh?" said Deuce.

"Could've been better," I admitted. "Most of it wasn't bad. Jammer's there. . . ."

"But . . . ?" said Deuce.

That's the thing about best friends: Sometimes they almost know you *too* well. I didn't really know what to say about that: *But they're older and like to give me a hard time? But one of them is a real Monster?* I'm not a whiner, and Mike and D wouldn't let me get away with it if I tried. I just changed the subject.

"Hey, Mike," I said. "Check the freezer and see if there are any Popsicles left."

Mike was the closest to the fridge. He always seemed to be.

"Sure, STAT," he said. STAT was a name my dad had given me a long time ago. It stood for Standing Tall and Talented. It was a nickname and kind of a reminder, too.

Mike ducked his head into the freezer and fished around for a while. Frosty white air drifted out around him. "Bad news," he said when he finally emerged. "Only two left."

"Yeah," I said, "and you've already taken a bite out of one of them!"

He looked down at the Popsicle in his hand. It had a corner missing and his lips were already bright red. "I couldn't help it," he said with a shrug. "Cherry's my favorite."

I let Deuce have the last one. We hung out for a little longer, and then they headed home. Afterward, I went to the freezer and pulled one last Popsicle out from behind a box of frozen vegetables. I always try to have a backup plan.

• • •

Speaking of backups, when it came time to head to practice number two on Sunday morning, I asked Junior if he'd drive me. I wasn't sure I could handle another long drive with Dad right now.

"All right," said Junior, "but hurry up. I don't want to be late for my job."

Everyone was working except me, but I had a job today, too. If I got another chance, I was going to try to dunk.

I wasn't sure it would work. I was still a good four inches away the last time I'd tried. I was hoping that big dinner and a good night's sleep would get me half of that and the embarrassment from yesterday would get me the rest.

Anyway, at least the ride over was better. We blasted the music and rode with the windows down.

CHAPTER 4

Practice began with some drills, a few too many wind sprints, and a lecture about "The Importance of Discipline" from Coach Dunn. To absolutely no one's surprise, the speech ran long. To make up time, we just went with the same teams as the day before for the scrimmage.

Right from the start, I had my hands full on defense. I wasn't the only one determined to do better in practice number two: Wayne was a real pain! He busted out a new move on their first possession. He got the ball down low, dribbled it a few times, and pump-faked. I bit on the fake just a little, but it was enough. He ducked his shoulder and slid past me like he'd been but-tered. His body went up and under. The ball went up and in.

As I turned to head up the court, I heard a low voice behind me.

"Pee-wee gets posterized!" Monster said.

"Just wait!" I said, turning my head and glaring at him. I was even more determined to try to dunk now.

"I got all day," Monster said with a wicked grin.

He was trying to get under my skin, and it was work-ing. I tried to shake it off. I had to keep my head in the game. I needed to find an opportunity to dunk — and the extra hops to do it. And I also had to figure out how to defend Wayne's low-post game.

I never got a chance to do either. The problem wasn't getting my head in the game — it was getting a finger in the eye! It happened on our next possession. Daniel hit me with a bounce pass, and Jammer set a screen for me near the baseline.

I didn't exactly agree that I'd been "posterized" by Wayne. They don't make posters of up-and-under moves. But I'd definitely been burned. I think Daniel and Jammer were giving me a chance to get that bucket back. Anyway, it was a good screen, and Wayne had a little trouble getting around it.

But the thing about screens is that people kind of bunch up around them. With this one, that meant Jammer's defender, my defender, and everyone else in the general area. And since we were in the paint, Monster was definitely in the area. He saw what was happening and sort of stuck his arm out to slow me down. His hand came up at the same time I ducked my head to start driving toward the rim.

One of his fingers went straight into my right eye. The last thing I saw was the tip of his finger. It looked huge because it was so close. It was like the world's least entertaining 3-D movie. And then the whole world went red and yellow and orange.

It hurt so much that I don't even remember falling down. I just realized I was on the ground at some point. I didn't even try to get up. Just pressed my hands down tight over my eye. I had a sick, weak feeling.

"You okay, man?" I heard in that familiar low voice.

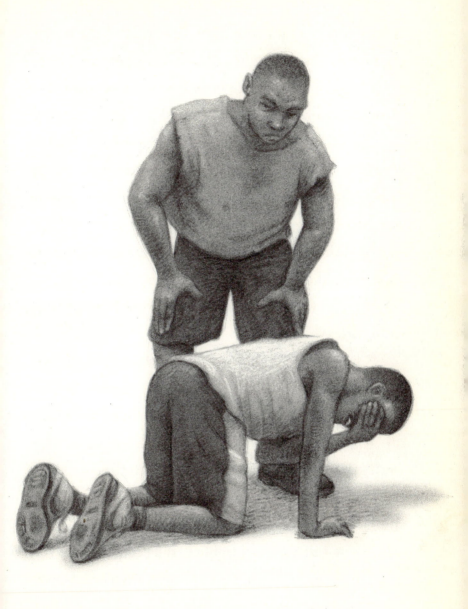

Even with my eyes shut tight I knew it was Monster. "Come on, kid, get up. You're all right."

His voice sounded different, but I didn't know how or why. My brain was buzzing too loud for me to really think. All I could do was sit there and hope my eye hadn't been poked out. More voices came toward me.

"Clear out! Clear out!" It was Coach Dunn. "Let me have a look!"

Next thing I knew, his voice was right beside me.

"How's it feel, Amar'e?" he said.

It felt awful, but I couldn't figure out how to tell him that.

"Can you see?" he asked. "How many fingers am I holding up?"

I managed to shake my head: no.

"Okay, take some time," he said.

I tried to calm down some. I still had that sick, panicky feeling, but I just sat there and breathed for a minute. That helped. The fireworks in my head were still going full force — bright swirling colors danced all around — but it didn't hurt as much anymore. Slowly, very slowly, I opened my left eye.

"Two fingers," I said.

The laser show in my head mixed with the view outside it in weird ways. Shooting stars flashed across the faces of the other players as they leaned in for a look.

"Yeah, that's good," said Coach. "But it's the other eye I'm interested in. Can you take your hands away?"

"Yes," I said, but my hands didn't budge.

"But?" said Coach.

"But I don't want to."

And I can't really explain it any better than that. My hand was pressed down tight, and slick with tears slipping out from under my eyelid. But part of me was thinking: *What if those aren't tears? What if it's really bad?* So, no, I wasn't taking my hands away.

Coach didn't insist. He just helped me up and started leading me off the court. I used my good eye to see where I was going as we headed toward the edge of the court.

"Where are we going?" I asked.

"The hospital!" he said.

CHAPTER 5

We didn't drive to the hospital so much as fly. Coach Dunn zoomed down the highway, swooping from lane to lane like a fighter plane. At one point, he asked for my dad's number. The thirty-second stretch it took him to make the call was the only time he slowed down at all.

The practice court was miles behind us by then. The rest of the kids had orders to "Shoot around or something — and don't get hurt!"

We arrived at the hospital in no time flat, and I was surprised that Dad was already there. He must've given that old truck a real talking-to. Coach said, "Good luck in there." Then he handed me off to Dad and left.

"Let's have a look," said Dad as we walked across the parking lot.

Maybe it was because it was my dad or because we were at the hospital now, or maybe I was just ready. Whatever the reason, I finally took my hand away from my right eye. Then, very slowly, I blinked it open. It stung when the air hit it, but not too bad. There were more stars and something seemed a little off, but I could definitely see. That was good news, at least.

"Hmmm," said Dad.

He didn't sound too happy, but he didn't seem too worried, either. I put my hand back over my eye, and we kept going. At the edge of the parking lot, there was a big sign over the sliding doors: EMERGENCY ROOM.

The doors shooshed open in front of us and closed behind us. Once we were inside, the emergency room turned out to be a lot less dramatic than I expected. I was thinking there'd be doctors and nurses running around and shouting, maybe someone being wheeled down the hall on a stretcher at a full run, like on TV. Instead, there was a whole lot of waiting going on.

I looked around with my good eye. A room full of people sat in plastic chairs waiting their turn. Some were holding their arms or wearing big bandages. Most of them had one or two people waiting with them, but some of them were just sitting there alone. One guy was coughing hard in a corner. There was a little ring of empty chairs around him.

We waited a long time and both looked a little out of place. I was dressed for hoops and Dad was in his green work clothes. We were both kind of sweaty when we sat down — me from the game and him from the job. But the air conditioner was turned up to "glacier," and we went from too hot to too cold in a hurry.

There was a little window in the wall with a nurse sitting at a desk behind it. Dad went up there a few times to ask how much longer it would be. The first time, I thought he was really worried about me. But then he went out in the hall to call his guys at the job site. He did that after his second trip to the little window, too. I started to get angry again. Was he worried about me, or about some guy's lawn?

"Better make sure the new guy hasn't mowed the

flower garden or watered the weeds," he said, getting up to make another call. It was a joke, but I wasn't laughing. After he came back, the nurse finally looked up from her desk and called my name.

Dad and I got up and walked through the little door. I took my hand away from my eye and even looked around with it a little as I walked. I figured if it fell out at this point, I was in the right place to have it put back in.

"The doctor will be right with you," the nurse said as she let us into a small white room. She left and closed the door behind her. Dad and I looked around. Things were starting to look more normal to me now. The place was so clean it shined, but I wondered how many people like the cougher in the corner had been in here already today.

There was a piece of paper on the wall called the *Pain Intensity Scale*. It was numbered from 0 to 10, with a little description of what each number meant. Beside zero it said *No pain*; beside ten it said *Worst pain imaginable*.

My eye still stung, and the area around it felt puffy, but it was probably only a two or three on that scale.

Before the doctor even came in, I decided not to complain about it. What if the last person in here was a ten? When the doctor arrived, he was a lot shorter than I expected. He was also a she.

"I'm Dr. Guntrum," she said, closing the door behind her. She sounded very businesslike. Before Dad or I could say our names, she added: "I understand you were poked in the eye."

I wasn't sure if I should say "Yes, ma'am," or "Yes, Doctor." Dad always insisted I address people the right way. "Yes, Doctor ma'am," I heard myself saying.

"Doctor will be fine," she said briskly. "Let me take a look."

She snapped on a pair of rubber gloves and got down to business. She had a good long look at my eye with some kind of magnifying device. Then she made me try to follow her finger and then a light. I could do most of what she asked me, but she still frowned the whole time. I think that was her default setting.

She put a little plastic paddle in front of my good eye so I could only use my hurt one. "What do you see?" she said.

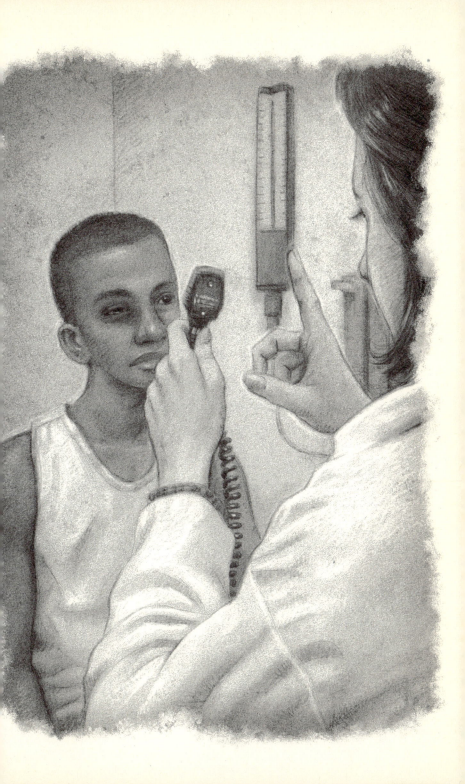

Since she was right in front of me, I said, "A doctor."

Her frown got bigger. "This happened during a basketball game?" she asked.

"Yes," I said. "It was an accident."

I'm not sure why I said that last part, but she didn't respond either way.

"How often do you play basketball?"

I wasn't sure why she was asking. She didn't seem like much of a hoops fan to me.

"Oh, he's always playing," said Dad behind me.

What did he mean by that? Did he mean playing instead of working? I wanted to turn around and see what kind of expression he had on his face, but the doctor was holding my chin with strong, cold fingers.

After that, they took me to another room to have my eye zapped with something that looked like a space laser. I don't know if it was an X-ray machine, a camera, a microscope, or what, but I was seeing a bright red dot for about ten minutes afterward.

Dad and I didn't say much, just went where Dr. Guntrum told us to. Dad always believed in letting people do their job. *She wouldn't tell me how to mow a lawn*, he would've said if I'd asked him about it.

Afterward, the doctor went off somewhere and sent us back to the little room to wait for the results.

Ten minutes later, she came in. She was holding a little plastic bottle in one hand and a small cardboard box in the other. She didn't close the door behind her this time, so I figured we'd be leaving soon. I was right. Dr. Guntrum stood there and rattled off the results with all the emotion of a teacher reading attendance. As she talked I tried to pick the important words out of her droning voice.

"Minor injury" seemed important. So did "take these eye drops before bed." But what she said after that didn't seem important as much as just weird. "You'll need to wear this eye patch" — she held up the little cardboard box — "unless you opt for safety goggles. Either way, you can't play basketball until I say so. . . . Any questions?"

You bet I had any questions.

"An eye patch?" I said.

She handed me the box, and I opened it. Inside was

a small black patch, shiny nylon on the outside and soft cotton on the inside, with maybe some plastic in between. I stretched out the black elastic strap.

"I have to wear this?" I said.

"You have to protect your eye until it heals," she said.

"But . . . ," I said. I couldn't figure out how to finish, but what I was thinking was: *How can I play basketball with one eye covered?*

Dad and the doctor both watched as I reluctantly put the patch on. The strap pinched my head a little, and it felt like my eye was in a dark cave. I looked up, feeling stupid. Dr. Guntrum must've seen my frown, because she said, "You can get safety goggles."

"What do you mean 'safety goggles'?" I asked.

"They look like glasses, and they protect your eyes."

"I know what they are, I just . . ." My voice trailed off. I'd seen some players wear them in the NBA, like in those old pictures of Kareem Abdul-Jabbar. But I'd never seen a kid wearing them.

"Where do we get them?" said Dad.

"You can order them on the way out," she said. "And you can have them delivered express."

"How long do I have to wear them?"

"Until your eye is better. You can come back in a week, and I'll take a look then."

"But a week from today is Sunday," I said. "I'll miss next weekend's practices."

"It may be more than a week," she said, as if I hadn't said anything at all. "I'll have to check my schedule."

"But those are the last practices before the tournament," I said.

Still no response. She really didn't get it.

"What can he do until then?" asked Dad.

"Normal activity," she said, turning toward him. "Just no contact sports."

"Basketball isn't a contact sport!" I blurted.

"Clearly, it was today," she said.

That made me so mad, I couldn't see straight. Or maybe that part was still from the poke in the eye. Either way, I was mad.

"But regular activities are okay?" said Dad.

"Yes," she said. "As long as your son avoids additional trauma to the eye, he can resume normal activity."

I wanted to shout, "Basketball is my normal activity!"

but they weren't even looking at me anymore. Dr. Guntrum left, and then we did, too. Dad had filled out a bunch of paperwork while we were waiting, but he had to fill out more on the way out.

I felt dumb and embarrassed standing there with my eye patch on. I adjusted the strap over and over again, just so people would know I didn't like the thing. Finally, Dad was done. I kept my head down on the way to the exit.

"Ordered those goggles," Dad said as the doors shooshed open in front of us. "Should be here Tuesday."

"Great," I said as the doors swept closed behind us. "I can't wait to stop looking like a pirate and start looking like a bug-eyed freak. I can't believe I can't play hoops until she says so!"

Dad looked over at me, deciding what part of that to answer. It wasn't even really a question. "At least you can do other things," he said after a few moments.

I remembered him asking the doctor about that. Then something occurred to me.

"Wait," I said. "Do you mean work?"

"What?" said Dad. I was too mad to wait for him to finish.

"You're glad this happened, aren't you? I can't play hoops, but I can sure help you work! That's what you meant in there, wasn't it?"

I couldn't believe it. But I remembered our long, silent trip to practice the day before, and then I could. I stormed ahead, but all I could do was climb into the truck and wait. Home was too far to walk, and I wasn't sure which direction to go, anyway.

"You're being ridiculous," Dad said as he climbed in his side.

I'm being ridiculous? I thought. *Take a look in the rearview mirror, Dad.*

I didn't say a word all the way home, I just looked out the window. Even with one eye covered, I could see a sunny day going to waste.

CHAPTER 6

Dad dropped me off at home and then headed back to work. Just a few minutes after he left, there was a knock on the door. *That's it, he changed his mind*, I thought. He wants me to "resume normal activity" behind a lawn-mower. But then I realized that Dad wouldn't knock on his own door. I got up to check it out.

"Hey, One Eye!" said Mike when I opened the door.

"What up, Cyclops?" said Deuce, standing next to him.

"How'd you find out?" I said.

"Small town," said Mike as I stepped aside to let them in. He had that right. Everyone pretty much knew everyone else's business down here in Lake Wales. They were both leaning in and looking at my eye patch.

"Not too bad," said Mike.

I figured he was just being nice.

"Kind of spy-ish," said Deuce. I figured he was pretending to agree. Then he added, "Let's have a look underneath."

I flipped up the patch and opened my eye as wide as I could so they could see. It still stung a little, and the sudden light made me blink. Once I stopped, things still looked a little off. All in all, it wasn't too bad. But I wasn't thinking about how it looked.

"Oh, man!" said Mike.

"That is red-eye times ten," said Deuce. "You look like a bad photo!"

"Gee, thanks," I said. "Nice to see you, too!"

"Least it's still in your head," said Mike.

"Is that supposed to make me feel better?" I said, but I felt better already, just having my friends there.

"Check it out, STAT," said Mike. He pulled a plastic case out of the big pocket of his cargo shorts.

I read the cover: *Air Scare*. It was a new fighter plane video game.

"Nice!" I said.

"Sure you can play in your, you know, condition?" said Mike.

"Yeah, no problem," I said. "I can beat you two with one eye tied behind my head!"

"I seriously hope *that* doesn't happen," said Mike.

I put my patch back on and really did play the game with one eye. I didn't win, though. Mike ruled the air that day, but he was cool about it.

After that, we went and sat in the folding chairs in the backyard. The afternoon had cooled down a little, and it was a nice day to just sit and talk about whatever. No surprise we wound up talking about hoops.

"Think we might have a tourney of our own coming up," said Deuce, nodding over toward Mike.

"Oh, yeah?" I said. These two were the main reason I started playing in tournaments myself.

"Yeah," said Mike, "it's two-on-two, just local stuff, down at the rec center."

"That sounds pretty cool," I said. "Maybe I'll come watch."

"Sure you can fit it into your calendar?" said Mike, a little smile appearing on his face. "Big star like you . . ."

Sometimes these guys busted on me about being invited to the bigger tournaments. I knew they were just joking, so I played along.

"Hey, I've always got time for the little people," I said, looking at Deuce, who was close to a foot shorter than Mike and me. "I'm not all me-me-me."

"No," said Deuce, pointing at my patch. "But today you're all eye-eye-eye!"

Deuce and I got a pretty good laugh out of that, but Mike didn't get it at first. That seemed even funnier, so we got a laugh out of that, too. Anyway, it was a nice afternoon, and I kind of needed it. Practices hadn't been going that great even before I got poked in the eye, with Monster calling me "Pee-wee" and all that. And then there was the thing with Dad.

Mike and Deuce took off an hour later. It was Sunday night, and we all had homework to finish up. Before they left, we made some plans.

"You guys want to hit the court this week?" I said.

"Thought you couldn't play until that grumpy doctor said so?" said Deuce.

"I can't play a real game: no contact," I said. "But I think I can do other stuff. And there's something I want to work on."

I'd been thinking about it. I had to miss the practices next weekend, but I was hoping I'd be back in time for the tourney. And I planned to return with a bang — and a dunk!

CHAPTER 7

I can sum up school on Monday in two words: pirate jokes.

"How arrrrrrrrr you?" asked Marcus, before the first bell even rang.

"You take the bus, or did the pirate ship drop you off?" said Tavoris.

And those guys were my friends! They dropped it once they heard what happened — and figured out how unfunny I thought it was. I wish I could say that for the rest of my class, or all the people who stared as they passed me in the hallway. Even Ms. Bourne got into the act in history class. She took the opportunity to tell us about all the famous pirates who operated off the coast of Florida back in the day.

History was my favorite subject, but I was seriously reconsidering that by the time she got to "the state's most famous pirate, José Gaspar." She said his pirate name was Gasparilla, and I was starting to wonder what mine would be.

Anyway, the day finally crept to an end. "Meet me at my place, okay?" I said to Mike and Deuce. "I've got an idea."

"Sure," said Mike.

"No problem," said Deuce.

But what they didn't say was just as important. Neither one made a single joke about my eye patch all day, not even when everyone else was and it would've been easy to join in. I can sum them up in two words, too: best friends.

Half an hour later, we were all assembled in my kitchen.

"What's the plan, STAT?" said Deuce.

Mike had his head in the fridge, as usual, looking to

see what he could scrounge. His hands were empty when he closed the door, but he was chewing on something.

"What?" he said when he saw me looking. "I'm a growing boy!"

I smiled and shook my head. I wanted to say something about how he was mostly growing around the waist, but it was time to get down to business. "I really want to work on my jumping," I said. "I can't play ball, but I figure I can do that. I thought maybe if I added some weights or something and really worked my legs. I want to get to where I can dunk!"

I thought I'd have to explain some more, but they both knew what I was talking about. "Yeah, I saw this thing on TV," said Mike. "It was about some wide receiver in the NFL and his crazy off-season workout. He ran sprints with a parachute strapped to his back, flipped over a giant truck tire, and stuff like that."

"Yeah, I saw one where a guy ran up and down a sand dune," said Deuce.

"Yeah," I said, "that kind of thing."

We all thought about it.

"Uh, anyone got a parachute?" Mike said after a while.

"No," I said, "and we're too far from the beach for a sand dune."

"You've got a backpack," said Deuce. "That's for sure."

"What's that got to do with anything?" asked Mike, but I'd already figured it out.

"Awesome idea, D!" I said.

The two of us headed to my room, with Mike a few steps behind. "What idea?" he said.

I picked my backpack up off the floor and dumped my school stuff out on my bed. Then I went to my bookshelf. I saw Mike watching, still trying to figure it out.

I found an old dictionary and a few other big books. I brought them back and stuffed them in my backpack. I put it on.

"What do you think?" said Deuce.

I jumped up and down a few times. "Pretty heavy," I said. "But there's more room."

Mike had figured it out by now. "Good idea," he said. "I was about to suggest that."

Deuce and I waved him off. Then we all looked around for a few more heavy objects. Deuce held up my work boots.

"Too bulky," I said.

Mike held up a bowling ball I got at a yard sale.

"You trying to kill me?"

He put it back where he'd found it and picked up my heaviest schoolbook.

"Might fall apart from all the jumping," I said.

Then we opened up the closet and found the mother lode.

"You keep your old notebooks?" said Deuce. "You're a bigger nerd than I am!"

"Well, I'm bigger, anyway," I said. But it was true. Years' worth of old school notebooks were stacked on the shelf of the closet. It was enough to fill up two backpacks. And just as I was thinking that, Mike pulled last year's backpack off the closet floor. He had a wicked smile on his face: "You can wear this one on front."

For a second, it seemed crazy, but then I started thinking about all the dunks I'd missed in practice. I remembered that layup, and Monster calling me Pee-wee. "Why not?" I said.

So we loaded both backpacks up, and I jumped up and down a few more times. It was definitely a good workout, but every time I landed, the notebooks slapped into me. "It kind of feels like there are people on both sides smacking me with books," I said.

"Now you know how school feels for me!" said Mike.

We laughed and then I started looking around the room. Deuce had thought of the first backpack, and Mike had thought of adding the second. It was my turn to come up with an idea. I spotted an old sweatshirt hung up in the closet.

"I just need some padding!" I said.

I took a few notebooks out, put the sweatshirt and a few old towels in, and I was good to go.

"All right, now that we've got a plan, you guys need to make sure I put in the work," I said. "I'm putting you guys in charge of the workouts, so I can't slack off. You good with that?"

"Oh, we're good," said Deuce.

"Definitely," said Mike.

They both had wicked grins on their faces. I slipped the backpacks off one at a time. "Can you help me carry this stuff to the park?"

Mike and Deuce looked at each other. "Nope," said Deuce, shaking his head. "Your training starts now!"

"Why do I get the feeling I'm going to regret making you guys my personal trainers?"

"That's enough lip," said Mike. "Load up and get moving!"

I groaned. I put the first backpack on my back and the second one on my front. Then I started walking. It felt like I had a baboon on my back and another one clinging to my front. This kind of thing looked so easy on TV!

We must've been quite a sight as we walked along the sidewalk in our little town: Mike and Deuce chatting and taking turns with the basketball, while I trudged along behind them wearing two backpacks and an eye patch.

Once we got to the park, I grabbed a seat on an old bench.

"What are you doing?" said Deuce.

"Resting," I said. "This stuff is heavy."

"Oh, you have so much to learn," said Deuce, shaking his head. "See those steps?"

I looked over at five flat stone steps with beat-up metal railings along each side. Sometimes you'd see older skateboarders on those steps — and sometimes you'd see them picking up their pieces at the bottom after a crash. "Yeah," I said, "so?"

"Well, start running," said Deuce.

"Oh, yeah," said Mike. "Running stairs. That was part of that receiver's workout, too. Course, he did it in a football stadium."

"Wish we had one of those," said Deuce.

I didn't!

"He can just run up and down these ones."

They were talking about me like I wasn't even there, but I guess that's what I'd asked them to do.

"How many times?" I asked.

"You let us worry about that," said Deuce. "Just get started."

I dragged myself to my feet. The packs were even

heavier than I remembered. I took my first trip up the stairs, and my legs and brain sent screaming signals back and forth with each step.

Brain to Legs: "Need more power for stairs."

Legs to Brain: "You have got to be kidding me!"

Brain to Legs: "I'm in charge here!"

Legs to Brain: "Says you?"

Brain to Legs: "Next step approaching!"

At first, my eye was a part of the conversation, too. With the patch on, it was harder for me to judge distances. I almost fell on each of the first few steps. But the steps were all the same distance apart, so after a while, I barely had to look at all.

I was running up the stairs okay — well, apart from all the work it required. But I couldn't run down. The pack in front felt like it was trying to pull me down the stairs, and the one in back felt like it was trying to push me down them.

"Uh, guys," I said. They were still deep in conversation, trying to decide how many sets I should do. I heard the word *hundred* float through the air. All I could do was hope there wasn't another number before it.

"Yeah?" said Mike.

"Think I need to walk down these things." I was about to explain why, but right then I stumbled a little and had to catch myself on the railing. They got the point.

"Okay," said Deuce. "Run up, walk down."

"Yeah," said Mike. "The eye patch is enough. You don't need crutches, too."

"How many times?" I said again.

"We're still working on that," said Deuce.

I shouldn't have been so worried about that. For one thing, I was the only one counting. For another, the next drill was even worse!

CHAPTER 8

By the time I got home from Day One of Operation Dunk, my legs felt like rubber. Junior gave me a funny look as I walked in the door, but I was too wiped out to even try to explain. I went into my room and stripped off the backpacks. (My "trainers" made me swear to wear them all the way home.) My sweat made them stick to my T-shirt.

I peeled the first one off: *THWUCK!*

The second one dropped to the floor: *SHWUNK!*

I gave them my best I-won't-miss-you look and headed out to the kitchen to drink about four years' worth of water. But a funny thing happened on the way to the kitchen. Even as dog-tired as I was, I had an extra spring in my step. After lugging those packs around all afternoon, walking without them felt so much easier. I actually felt lighter.

When I got to the kitchen, Junior already had a big glass of lemonade on the table waiting for me. I drank the whole thing without even looking up — or wondering why my brother was being so nice. Was it because of my eye injury?

"Looks like you had a killer workout," he said. That was why: He'd had plenty of long, tough workouts himself. He knew the deal.

"I put my friends in charge," I said.

"Ouch," he said. "That was brave."

"Or dumb!" I said. We both laughed, and I headed to the fridge for some water. I flipped my eye patch up after that. I wasn't going to get hit by anything in our own kitchen — and I needed to let it dry off underneath. In Florida, everything sweats!

Dad was still working long hours, and he got home late again that night. He didn't say much at the dinner table, so I decided to fill the silence by telling him about my crazy practice.

"You should've seen him," said Junior. "I barely rec-ognized him under the backpacks, eye patch, and twelve gallons of sweat."

Dad looked from Junior to me, his fork halfway between his plate and his mouth. He shook his head slowly. "Must be nice," he said. "Playing around all afternoon."

My stomach dropped. It was like he hadn't even heard us, about the backpacks and all the sweat. "I worked hard!" I said.

Dad took a slow bite, then said: "Worked at playing, maybe."

That made me so mad, I couldn't figure out how to respond. "But . . . I . . . didn't," I started. Yep, that defi-nitely wasn't it.

"You aren't even supposed to be playing basketball yet," he said.

"I wasn't playing," I said. "I was practicing!"

He gave me a look, like: *Come on now.*

But it wasn't the same thing! No one was going to elbow me in the eye when I was running up stairs. It felt like he was intentionally missing the point. He was doing that Dad thing: *Now, son, is that really the smartest decision?*

I looked right at him. He'd washed up for dinner, but he hadn't had the energy to change out of his work clothes yet. I opened my mouth to say something, but I just closed it again. There was no way I was going to win this argument. It was his house, his table, his rules. And as hard as I'd worked today, he'd worked harder.

We ate the rest of the meal in silence.

I headed to my room after dinner to get my homework out of the way. At least Dad couldn't lecture me about that. It was a little distracting to read with the eye patch on, so I took it off. It felt good to have that elastic band off my head, and I figured it was okay. My eye felt a lot better now. I understood why I still had to protect it, that just because it didn't hurt didn't mean it was healed. I made a mental note not to stick my pencil in it and got to work. I'd made it through English and half of math when the phone rang.

"Hey, STAT," called Junior. "It's for you."

I got up to head for the house phone in the hall. At the last second, I remembered to grab my eye patch and put it back on. Dad would probably be mad if he saw me without it. He was the one who had to pay the doctor bills.

"Hello?" I said after Junior handed me the phone.

"S'up, player?" I heard. It took me a few moments to recognize the voice. We'd exchanged numbers weeks ago, but this was the first time he'd called.

"Hey, Jammer! Not much. What about you?"

"Staying out of trouble," he said.

"I doubt it."

He laughed and said, "How's the eye, man? Looked like a pretty nasty poke."

"Not too bad. Rockin' an eye patch," I said. Before he could make a pirate joke, I added the first thing I could think of: "Supposed to get goggles, maybe tomorrow."

"For real?" he said. "How long do you have to wear those things?"

"Not sure. It's up to the doctor. I hope it's not too long. In the picture I saw, they were big, bug-eye-looking things. And the dude they had wearing them: not cool."

"Yikes, that's rough," said Jammer. "But we all know you've got more style than that guy. Guess I'll see on Saturday."

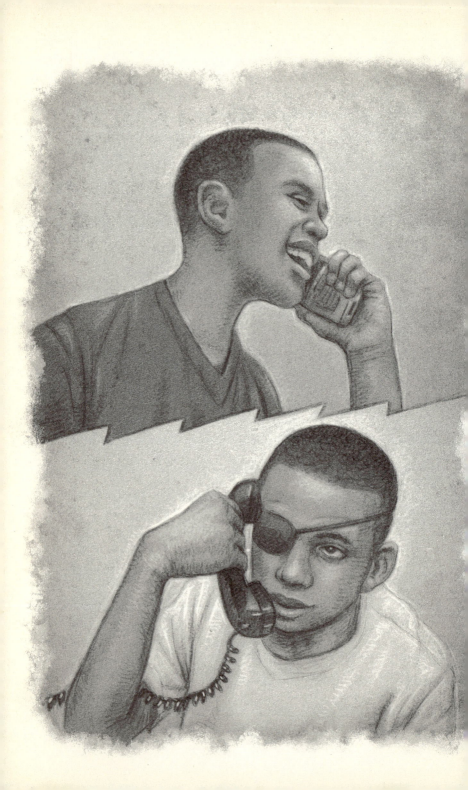

"I wish," I said. "Have to wait till the doctor gives me the go-head, and my appointment's not until Monday."

"Aw, man," said Jammer. "Not cool."

"Seriously."

"That's the last weekend of practice before the tourney," he said.

"Believe me, I know. I've just got to practice on my own and try to be ready."

"Okay, well, good luck, man," he said. "Guess I'll see you at the tourney."

"Definitely." I said, even though it wasn't technically up to me.

"I'll let the guys know how you're doing," he said.

"Yeah, say what up to Khalid and them for me," I said. "And poke Monster in the eye."

We had a good laugh at that one. I passed Dad on my way back to the second half of my math homework. "Who was that?" he asked.

"My teammate," I said. I was glad to have a teammate like Jammer. I just wished I could get back on the court with him already.

CHAPTER 9

*T*he pirate jokes were already dying down on Tuesday. There were a few "arrr"s here and there and a few kids acting like they had a peg leg or hook hand or whatever. But I was bigger than most of them, had good friends, and the patch actually looked kind of tough. All in all, the age of piracy was coming to a close. I wouldn't miss it.

At lunch, Mike and Deuce wanted to talk about Day Two of training. Give your friends a chance to boss you around and you can bet they'll talk about it at the lunch table! I had to smile as Deuce told Tavoris and Marcus about his "genius idea" with the first backpack and Mike chimed in about his idea to "double-down" with the second.

"Yeah," bragged Deuce, "we've got something tough in store for him today."

"All right, hold up," I said. "First up, I'm right here, so why are you talking like I'm still in gym? And second, it'll have to wait. I've got something I have to do after school today."

The look on Deuce's face when I told him that: You would've thought I'd just taken away his only toy. He tried to hide his disappointment by turning to Mike. "Sounds like our workouts are too extreme for him," he said.

"You wish," I said.

"Then why are you afraid of a little work?" said Mike.

"I'm not," I said. "I'll be doing plenty of work today."

And I would, too. I'd never been afraid of hard work or extra effort. I was just a little surprised that I still had to prove it. I headed home after school to change and get ready. When I got there, I saw something leaning up against the front door. It was a small cardboard box.

Looks like the UPS man has been here, I thought as I picked it up. I was surprised to see that it was addressed to me.

For a split second, I was excited. Who doesn't like to get a mysterious, gift-size package delivered to them out of the blue? It was like a little piece of Christmas morning. And then I remembered: *It's Tuesday, just like the doctor said. It's the darn goggles.*

I ripped open the cardboard with my hands like I was mad at the box. They were inside, all packed up in bubble wrap. I lifted them out and looked at them. The goggles seemed to be looking right back at me, like some two-tailed, jumbo-eyed fish. *You've got to be kidding me*, I thought. And then I saw the note: *Wear these until our next appointment — including at school!*

It was signed with the kind of squiggly scrawl that was on every doctor's note I'd ever seen. I was pretty sure I saw a *G* in there, so I knew it was from sour, dour Dr. Guntrum. I was surprised she didn't just sign it with a frowning face.

I tried to imagine what the kids at school would say. My school could be pretty rough on kids with glasses.

If anybody could pull these things off, it was me, but I didn't have time to figure this out right now. I put the goggles back in the box, took the box to my room, and stuffed it under my bed. Then I changed into some old jeans and a T-shirt, hopped on my bike, and headed off toward the edge of town.

There were a few office parks out there, and I knew that Dad and his crew were working at one of them. I knew I'd found the right one when I heard the sound of the big riding mowers and saw his truck parked at the edge of the parking lot.

I thought about leaving my bike in one of the parking spots. I thought it would be kind of funny. Those spots were for people who worked here, and I planned on working. But some dude would probably just pull his Honda in without looking and my bike would be roadkill. I leaned it against a tree and went to find Dad. He called his riding mower a "lawn tractor," and he was so surprised to see me, he nearly fell right off it.

"What are you doing here, STAT?" he said, killing the engine. "You okay? The eye bothering you?"

"Nah, I'm all right," I said. I thought about telling

him the goggles had arrived, but he'd just want to know why I wasn't wearing them. "I just thought I'd help out."

I didn't usually help out during the week. Dad always made it clear that my main job then was getting good grades at school. But then I didn't usually get accused of goofing off and only "working at playing" at dinner. I usually worked on the weekends, but I'd been missing those lately, too, because of basketball practices.

"What's your homework situation?" Dad asked.

"I'm all caught up. Just a few little things for tonight."

"And your eye?"

"Feels all right. Should be fine under the eye patch."

He looked at me carefully, considering it. I don't know if he knew I was there to prove a point — or if he thought I was there because he'd proven his. But as busy as he was, he wasn't about to turn down an extra pair of hands. "Okay," he said at last. "Go help Manny over there, but tell him no power tools. I don't think the vibrations would be good for that eye."

He didn't smile or say thanks, and he definitely didn't apologize. I'd missed whole days of work and now I was showing up for the last few hours of this one. But he gave me a little nod, and that felt like something. I went to find Manny as Dad's lawn tractor roared back to life behind me.

Manny was in the big garden out front. The company that owned the office park had its name spelled out in bright flowers facing the highway. The whole thing was surrounded by carefully trimmed bushes and shrubs. It was the kind of job you had to be careful with so you didn't end up putting a foot-shaped dot in the wrong part of the *i*.

Manny was kneeling down in the flower bed, so I could only see his back. I knew it was him, though. He'd worked with us for years. "Hey, Manny," I said. "Dad says I should give you a hand. Just no power tools, 'cause of my eye."

"Oh, yeah," he said, standing up and turning around. "I heard about that. How's it feeling?"

I just shrugged. I'd been answering questions about my eye for days now, and it was getting old, but that wasn't why I didn't answer him. The reason for that: I was too busy looking at his safety goggles. He wore them when he was trimming hedges or pruning

69

trees. Any time a branch or thorn might poke him in the eye. I guess I was so used to seeing them that I hadn't even thought about that. They looked so much like the ones that came today that I wondered if they were the same brand.

"Earth to Amar'e," he said.

"Yeah, sorry, Manny," I said, snapping back to the here and now.

"Get some gloves and start pulling weeds," he said. "We got some sneaky ones trying to take over the *S* over there. Think there might be something going on with the *E*, too."

"Got it," I said.

I headed over to Dad's truck to get some gloves and his hedge clippers. As I walked, I took one more look back at Manny's goggles.

I worked a good three hours: weeding, trimming, clipping, and whatever else Manny needed me to do. When we were done, I threw my bike in the back of Dad's truck and we headed home. The truck was running even worse than the last time I was in it. There was

one uphill where I was thinking, *This would be quicker on the bike.*

Dad was still in a bad mood, but I think it was mostly about the truck. He didn't really say anything about me showing up to work. He didn't really say anything about anything. When we turned onto our block, I finally asked: "You ever wear safety goggles, like Manny?"

"Sure," he said. His voice flat and tired. "I've got a pair somewhere. Just depends on the job."

"Hmm," I said.

It was definitely something to think about. And I did, too. But when I headed to school the next day, I had my eye patch on. The goggles were still stuffed under my bed.

Depends on the job, he'd said. My assignment today was sixth grade. It just didn't seem like big, bug-eyed glasses were the right tool for the job.

CHAPTER 10

Wednesday was business as usual at school: a pop quiz here, a spelling test there. No one even mentioned the eye patch.

Right before lunch I heard a low voice behind me: "I hope you enjoyed your day off!" I should've known it was Deuce. He was making his voice sound like the drill sergeant he thought he was.

"Some day off," I said. "I must've pulled up half the weeds in Florida."

"That's highly unlikely," he began. "In the Everglades alone there are . . ." And then he caught himself and went back into Super Trainer mode. "I mean, you're going to wish you were pulling weeds today! We're going to do twice as many stairs, and I have something new planned, too."

"Oh, great," I said. I could feel those backpacks on me already.

A few hours later, I was getting ready to put them on for real. I was swapping out the textbooks in my school pack for the heavy load of old notebooks and other stuff. Before I put it on, I bent down and stuck my hand under my bed. I fished around until I found the box with the goggles.

I took them out and looked at them. I guessed it wouldn't be so bad to wear them to the park. There was hardly anyone there during the week, anyway, and I really didn't like the way the patch got all sweaty. I put the goggles on. It was nice to be able to see with both eyes.

Right on cue, I heard Mike knocking on the door. I could tell it was him because he always knocked too hard. I walked out to the kitchen wearing both backpacks and the goggles. Mike and Deuce had gone easy on me with the eye patch, but I was sure they'd bust on me for the goggles.

"Cool goggles, man," said Deuce.

I was happy to be wrong again.

"Yeah, you look old school," said Mike. "Like Kareem Abdul-Jabbar."

"Yeah, definitely," said Deuce. "Maybe we should work on your skyhook."

I expected them to make fun of me, and instead they'd compared me to a Hall of Famer. They definitely weren't as nice once we got to the park. I always knew Deuce was smart. I mean, the guy knew how many weeds there were in the Everglades! But it turned out he was a legit genius when it came to finding ways to make me work my legs.

We started off with the two drills from the first day. First up (and down) was running that little set of stairs. Deuce was true to his word and had me do twice as many, but it was easier with the goggles. I could judge distances better with both eyes on the job, so I could run down the stairs, too. I did twice as many in the same amount of time. I was feeling like a beast until Deuce said, "Good, now you have time to do twice as many jumps onto the bench."

They had me jumping on and off this bench. It felt like eight years, but they claim it was only ten minutes. Mike was timing me with his mom's plastic egg timer, and I was fried and scrambled by the time it went off. "Okay, you're done," he said.

"I'm done in!" I said. "Water break."

I started trudging toward the old water fountain before they could say no. My backpacks flopped against my sweaty shirt with each step. When I'd had about a gallon's worth, I headed back. Mike and Deuce were standing on the basketball court now.

"Over here," called Deuce. "Stand right under the rim."

"Okay," I said once I was right under the ratty old net.

"Now jump up and touch it," said Deuce.

"The net?" I said.

"The rim."

"I can't touch the rim," I said. "I've got two stuffed backpacks on."

"You can't touch it anyway," said Deuce. Ouch. "That's why we're here. Just get as close as you can."

Man, that was humbling. I stretched my right arm

and hand up as high as they could go, but I could barely even get off the ground with those backpacks on. My first jumps were the best, but even then there was some serious airspace between my fingers and the rim. I could see it right above me, though. The rim *looked* close enough to touch. It was like it was taunting me. It was good motivation, and probably a good workout, but pretty soon I was done.

"That's it, guys," I said. *"No más."*

They looked at each other and nodded.

"I'm glad you two are satisfied," I said. "Especially since you haven't sweated one drop today!"

"Hey," said Deuce. "We are *sacrificing* our own work-outs to help you!"

"That's right," said Mike. "We're heroes!"

If I'd had the energy to laugh, I would've. Instead, I slipped out of my bags and left them on the ground as I stood up. My legs were definitely tired, but I had that weird weightless sensation, too. My body felt so much lighter without the extra load. I looked up at the rim, still right above me. I guess I had one more jump in me. I knelt down and sprung straight up. And you know what? I almost made it. Even without a running start, my fingertips came pretty close to the iron. Which was good, since a running start was completely out of the question now.

"Pretty close," said Mike.

"Yeah, you're definitely getting there," said Deuce.

I couldn't believe it. I looked at my friends. As crazy as their methods were, they were onto something. We chilled out for a while, and I got some more water. My legs still felt like wet noodles, but pretty soon I felt good enough to shoot around a little. After a few shots, I heard voices. A group of older kids was heading for the other side of the court.

For a second, I thought about my goggles. I wondered what these older kids would think. But I didn't sweat it too much. (I didn't have that much sweat left!) Deuce and Mike thought they were okay, and I didn't even know these other kids. Plus, the goggles seemed right for a basketball court. That's where I hurt my eye in the first place.

We shot around until it was time to go. The older kids didn't say anything about my goggles. Maybe they didn't notice. Anyway, my shot was falling. I hadn't dunked yet, but at least I could still put it in the old-fashioned way.

I didn't want to put the sweaty backpacks back on afterward, but it was the best way to get them home. Plus, my trainers insisted. I was really dragging by the time I reached the yard. Sure enough, Dad was right there unloading his truck. It was too late to take the packs or the goggles off, and I was too tired, anyway.

He looked over at me. I wondered if he was going to say something about me goofing off again, working at playing and all that stuff. His mouth was pinched down into a frown, and it looked like he was considering it. But when he spoke, all he said was: "About time those goggles arrived. Ordered them on Sunday."

"Yep," I said, and shuffled into the house before he could change his mind.

CHAPTER 11

I got up a little early on Thursday. I'd decided to wear the goggles. No one had said anything bad about them yet, and I'd always been pretty confident about my style. But part of my brain was still saying, *Don't do it! Just wear the patch. Kids are used to it now.* I told that part of my brain to pipe down and get back to picking clothes. If I was going to do this, I was going to do it with a super-fresh outfit.

I stood in front of my dresser and asked myself: *What goes with goggles (other than swim fins)?* I tried on some different things. Finally, I came up with the perfect combination: my best jeans, crisp kicks, and a cool sweater. Yep, it was the kind that buttoned down the

front. If kids were going to call me a nerd because of the goggles, I'd be the coolest nerd they'd ever seen.

Once I got to school, I spotted Deuce in the hallway. I walked up behind him and said, "All right, man, be honest. What do you think?"

He spun around. "Okay, STAT, seriously, a guy as big as you shouldn't be sneaking up on us little dudes," he said. "Second, let me have a look."

He put his hand under his chin, like he was deciding whether or not to buy a car. Not that a twelve-year-old can buy a car, but you get the idea. "Mm-hmm," he said.

"What?" I said.

"Fresh," he said.

"Yeah?"

"Yeah."

"It's not too much?" I said, hooking a finger under the front of my sweater.

"On me it would be," he said. "But if anyone can pull that look off, it's you.

"Besides," he added, "you're too big to be a nerd."

We headed to homeroom. From this point on, confidence was the key.

Did you ever get something really cool that you just couldn't wait to show off? Like maybe your favorite player's jersey or an awesome pair of new sneakers, and you couldn't wait until you got into school so everyone could see? Well, that's how I acted with the goggles. I held my head up high — which was saying something at my height — and walked with confidence. I was just like, *All right, homeroom, check out my new goggles.*

A girl named Lucy stared right at them as I headed for my desk. I could see she didn't know what to think. So I looked right back at her and gave her a nod and a little smile. "Pretty cool, right?" I said.

The whole room was watching now.

She smiled.

"Yeah, you're looking good today, Amar'e," she said.

The whole room looked at me again: the goggles, the outfit, my head and shoulders held up high.

"Are those glasses?" asked my friend Marcus.

"Nah, they're goggles," I said. "To protect the eye I hurt playing hoops."

"Like the eye patch?" said a kid named Joey.

"Yeah, except I can see the whole room now."

"Cool," said Marcus.

"I've seen those on NBA players," said Joey.

That pretty much sealed the deal. I kept it up all day: not just wearing the goggles but kind of showing them off. It worked. By last period, a few kids even asked me where they could get a pair like mine.

"I know this lady," I said, thinking of sour-faced Dr. Guntrum, "but it's kind of a pain to get in to see her."

Mike and Deuce cracked up, but no one else got it. I laughed, too. I was feeling pretty good about things — except for my legs, which still felt like Jell-O from the workout yesterday. And as the final bell rang, I knew I wasn't about to get a break.

"All right, private," said Deuce, switching immediately into drill sergeant mode. "We'll see you at the court. I suggest you lose that sweater."

With the goggles on, the whole class could see me roll my eyes.

We practiced hard on Thursday and Friday. It seemed like it was working. My muscles were definitely screaming at me, but I wasn't sure exactly how much it was helping my jumping. We did the drill where I tried to touch the rim from a standing jump both days, but there was no way I was going to get there with those backpacks on. And by the time I took them off, my legs were too fried.

I really looked forward to just shooting around at the end. And yeah, I would've looked forward to pretty much anything that didn't involve sweltering under double-barreled backpacks at that point. But shooting around was especially sweet. It was nice to just drift around the court with the packs off, nailing J's, and letting the breeze cool me down after all that hard work.

I was sure that none of the other kids who'd be playing in the tournament were working harder than I was. I felt good about that. Maybe not when I was on my fiftieth set of stairs, or when I woke up in the morning with my legs tied in knots. But at the end of practice, when I faded away and drained a fifteen-foot jumper? Yeah, that felt good.

I'd need it, too. Tomorrow and Sunday, those other kids would be practicing hard. The coach would be watching every move and giving them pointers. Monster would be patrolling the paint like a chained dog, and

Jammer would be rising above it all. And me, I'd be pushing a lawn mower or pulling up weeds. I'd already made up my mind: Practice hard all week and help out Dad on the weekend. I could still picture him looking at me with that big, fat frown the other day, and it bothered me.

Deuce doubled the number of times I had to run up and down the stairs again on Friday. "Come on, D," I said. "I've been doing this all week."

"You're the one taking the weekend off to work," he said.

"Taking the weekend off to work?" I said. "That doesn't even make any sense!"

But he was having none of it. "Get going before I double it again," he said. He was enjoying this way too much, but I got going.

CHAPTER 12

I worked all Saturday. I really could've used a day off after the week I'd had. Weren't people supposed to relax on the couch or something like that when they were injured? Instead, I felt like I'd been going twice as fast and doing twice as much since the moment I got back from the hospital.

"Well, look who's here," said Dad when I climbed into the truck on Saturday morning. I didn't know what he meant by that, and once we got going it was almost too loud to ask. The engine rumbled and coughed. The backfires had gone from firecrackers to thunder-cracks. I was almost surprised we made it to the job.

I went over to help Manny again — and we were wearing almost the same goggles. He shook his head and I smiled. "Don't be biting my style now, Amar'e," he said.

At the end of the day, Dad and I climbed in the truck and just sat there.

Manny left.

The other guys left.

Some dude who was at the office park working on a Saturday left.

And we watched them go. It seemed like a bad idea: What if the truck didn't start? Or blew up? But that's not why I was nervous. I was nervous because we were pretty clearly going to Have A Talk. He was facing forward with his hands on the steering wheel like a little kid pretending to drive.

"I was thinking," he said to the windshield. "The other day, when you came into the yard with those backpacks on and a ball in your hands."

Here we go, I thought. *He's going to let me have it about the basketball. He's so mad he can't even look at me.*

"You know what I was thinking, STAT?"

I looked straight ahead, too. The cab of the truck felt small and hot.

"Nope," I said.

"I was thinking: He is working hard."

I wasn't sure I heard him right. I looked over at him, but he was still talking to the windshield. "He may not be mowing lawns, but he's a kid. He's got something that's important to him, and he's working hard at it."

I could've said something. I could've jumped up and said, "I told you so!" But for one thing, if you jump up in a truck, you're just going to hit your head. And for another, this wasn't a time to talk. My dad was a proud man, and he was apologizing, in his own way. The thing to do was to keep my lips zipped and let him finish.

"And he's your son, and you should be proud of him."

Dad was a big man with a big voice, but he said these last words so quietly I barely heard them: "And I am." And then he turned the key and the truck sputtered a few times and roared to life.

"Thanks, Dad," I said, but I don't know if he heard me over the rumbling. I lifted my goggles and wiped

something from under my eyes. Some sweat must've collected under there or something.

I woke up sore all over on Sunday. My legs were still screaming from a week of workouts and the rest of me was yelping from a full day of weeding and mowing. At least I didn't have to garden with those backpacks on, I thought. And then I listened a little closer and knew I wouldn't have to garden at all — not with all that rain beating down on the roof!

I could do anything I wanted today. I started it out with another hour of sleep. I don't think I was the only one, either. I didn't hear a single sound in the house apart from the rain on the roof. At least, I didn't hear anything in the 3.5 seconds it took me to fall back to sleep.

When I woke up again, it was still raining. I heard voices out in the living room, so I thought I'd better get up and see what was going on. Dad was standing there looking out the window, carrying a big mug of coffee. It was dark gray outside, but it was like a cloud had lifted between the two of us now. He was wearing his worn-out old bathrobe over his work pants and a white T-shirt.

He must've been half-dressed before he realized the rain wasn't going to let up.

Junior was sitting on the couch with a plate in front of him and a video game controller in his hand. The plate was empty but I could tell from the thin layer of syrup on it that he'd had waffles.

We all looked at each other and said "Mornin'" at exactly the same time. I guess when you live with people long enough, you get into the same rhythm. I headed into the kitchen to get some waffles of my own and came back out to school Junior on whatever game he was playing.

It was a nice, lazy morning. The rain stopped for a while, and I thought Dad might try to get some work in after all. He didn't look too disappointed when it started back up again. "Grow, grass, grow," he said. Rain was always good news for the owner of a lawn care company. "That's what I call 'business development.'"

"How's it going?" said Junior.

I never really asked Dad about work, but sometimes Junior did. I guess because he was older and had a real after-school job of his own.

"Good," said Dad. "Been busy" — no kidding, I thought — "but we're just about done at that big old office park, and it'll settle down some after that."

"Done for now," said Junior, nodding toward the rain.

"Yes, indeed," said Dad. "And I think they'll have us back before too long. And they say money doesn't grow on trees. . . ."

"Yeah," said Junior. "Maybe then you'll be able to afford a new bathrobe!"

Dad raised his right arm. A big hole appeared underneath it, and he looked at us through the hole. "What's wrong with this one?" he said.

It was fun to joke around with my dad and brother again, but it kind of made me miss the rest of my family. After a while, I headed into the next room to call my mom and half brother up in New York. It was a regular Sunday thing for me, so I figured I'd just call a little early.

Afterward, I came back into the room to get Junior so he could talk, too. Dad's bathrobe was nowhere in sight, and he had his shirt and shoes on. I looked out the window. It wasn't raining as hard, but it was still coming down.

"You aren't working, are you?" I asked.

"Nah," said Dad. "But I am taking care of my most important piece of equipment."

"The lawn tractor?"

"The truck, STAT," he said. "Called first thing this morning and got an appointment. Finally getting that old bucket of bolts fixed up."

That reminded me of my own appointment tomorrow: at the doctor's. A little explosion of nerves went off inside me. My bucket of bolts wasn't that old, but what if there was still something wrong with my right headlight?

"Headed downtown if you want to come along," said Dad.

"Sure," I said. "At least if the truck catches fire today the rain will put it out."

The truck lurched and coughed all the way to the garage. Dad talked to the mechanic for a while, and then we watched as he raised the whole truck up on the hydraulic lift. Before he started working, he put on goggles, too.

"Don't be biting my style," I said.

We got some lunch downtown while we waited. Neither of us was surprised when the mechanic said they had to keep the truck overnight. Dad just called Junior, and he came and picked us up in his car.

It was a good day, and the best part? I didn't miss practice. There's no way they were out there today — not unless they planned to switch the basketball tournament to a swim meet.

CHAPTER 13

By Monday, everyone was used to the goggles. Sometimes I even forgot I had them on. Then the final bell of the school day went off like the horn at the end of a basketball game. Today was going into overtime, though. I finally had my appointment with Dr. Guntrum to see how my eye was doing. I was hoping she'd say it was all healed up and I was good to go for the tournament. My eye seemed okay. I could see fine and the area around it wasn't swollen anymore. But sometimes it still felt a little uncomfortable, like when an eyelash gets stuck under your lid. It wasn't so red anymore, but what did I really know about eyes? And what about the parts I couldn't see?

Anyway, I must've been nervous about it, because when that final bell went off I jumped about two feet. That was pretty impressive considering I was sitting down at the time.

"Good luck," said Deuce as we gathered up our books and got ready to head home. He knew the deal.

Ten minutes after I got home, I was in the kitchen fixing myself a snack when Dad walked in the door. He kind of surprised me. (Okay, I admit it: I jumped another two feet.) "I didn't even hear you pull in," I said.

"That's right," he said, smiling. "The truck's a whole lot quieter now."

I looked out the window and there it was in the driveway. Two days ago, I would've heard it coming a quarter mile away.

"Thing's like a stealth fighter," I said.

I hoped things would go as well with my appointment. And then something else occurred to me, and I just about dropped my sandwich. That truck didn't fix itself. . . . What if I still wasn't better and they had to operate on me?

"Well," said Dad, "we might as well get this over with."

I thought we'd have to go back to the emergency room and wait again. I wasn't looking forward to spending another long stretch in that sad, germ-filled waiting room. It turned out I didn't need to. Dad parked on the other side of the hospital this time, and we walked in the big front doors.

"Where are we going?" I asked.

"We've got an appointment this time," he said. "We're going to her office."

"You mean Dr. Guntrum?"

"Yep," he said.

I just nodded. I kind of wished it was with someone a little less serious and gloomy. I ended up in a different waiting room this time. From what I could tell so far, hospitals seemed to be about half made up of waiting rooms. This one was smaller, though, and everyone waiting inside was a kid. Some of them were a little younger than me, and some of them were a little older, but at least none of them were sitting in a corner and coughing nonstop.

I looked over at Dad, sitting next to me. It was amazing to me that we'd been so mad at each other. Families are funny that way. It's like they're equal parts hurt feelings, short memories, and forgiveness. And just when I was thinking about all these big things, the nurse called my name. Or something like my name. She mispronounced it pretty badly, but when no one named "Ay-meer-ay" stood up, I knew it was me.

Dad and I got up and headed into another little room. It looked almost exactly like the little room from last time, even though I was in a completely different part of the hospital. I looked around once the nurse closed the door behind us. Sure enough, there was my old friend the Pain Intensity Scale.

We only waited a few minutes, but with every one that passed, I was more sure it was going to be bad news. Things had been going too well lately, and this is where it all went wrong.

But then the weirdest thing happened. Dr. Guntrum came into the room, and she was *smiling*! I could hardly believe it. I looked all around, but I couldn't see that dark cloud that had been over her head anywhere.

"All right, Amar'e," she said. "Let's take a look at that eye."

She even pronounced my name right.

"How were the goggles?" she asked.

Did she say were? I thought.

"Fine," I said.

"All right, well, take them off now so I can get a better look."

I took the goggles off and handed them to Dad. She took out a tiny flashlight and made me follow it with my eyes. Then she shined it in the right one. Basically, she did the same stuff as last time, but she was still smiling. I wanted to ask, "Who are you, and what have you done with Dr. Guntrum?" but she was the one asking the questions.

"How does it feel?" she said.

"Okay," I said.

"No pain?"

"Just a little sometimes," I said. I told her about the eyelash thing.

"Mm-hmm," she said.

She flipped up my eyelid and looked underneath. "A-ha," she said, as if she'd found a gold coin under there. The rubber glove she'd put on made her hand feel cold.

"All right," she said, taking a few steps back and snapping the glove off her hand. "I'm going to give you something else, a cream this time. You put it right under that top eyelid, morning and night. Let's say a week."

Dad and I started talking as soon as she stopped.

"What about basketball?" I asked.

She looked at me. "Play ball!" she said.

All right! I pumped my fist to celebrate.

I liked this version of Dr. Guntrum a lot better than the one in the emergency room. I guess the emergency room wasn't exactly smile central.

"But wear the goggles for another couple of weeks, just when you play," she added. "And try not to hurt yourself."

"He won't," said Dad, handing the goggles back to me. "He's more coordinated than he looks."

They both thought that was pretty funny.

"Well, you better clear out," said Dr. Guntrum. "There's a nine-year-old with a projectile vomiting problem coming in next."

Dad and I got out of there like we had rockets on our

feet, but not before I said one more thing. "Thank you, Dr. Guntrum."

"You're welcome," she said.

And I wasn't just saying it, either. I really was thankful. I was thankful and relieved and, most of all, ready to play some basketball!

CHAPTER 14

"Hey, guys," I said at lunch on Tuesday. "Who's up for some hoops after school?"

Deuce looked over. "What about the workouts?" he asked.

"Not today, D," I said. "I need to get out on that court and operate."

"You know I'm game," said Deuce.

Mike just nodded. Of course he was in. But we still needed one more for two-on-two, and Marcus and Tavoris both said they were busy.

"What about you, Dougie?" I said.

"I've got some things to do," he said.

"Come on, man," I said. "I haven't played in forever."

He looked over at me for a few seconds, considering it. Then he broke into a little smile. "I guess I can do them later on," he said. "I'm in."

"Great!" I said.

We had our four. A few hours later, we were walking onto the court. If our team had been sponsored by a local business, like in Little League, it would've been an optician. I had my goggles back on for the game, just like the doctor ordered. And Dougie showed up wearing his own pair of goggles!

"Where'd you get those?" I said.

"My pops had an extra pair for work," he said as we bumped fists. I knew exactly what he meant.

"I just thought it was kind of a cool look," he added. "And I don't want anything happening to these soulful brown eyes of mine."

"Well, it makes picking teams easy," said Mike.

"Oh, yeah," said Deuce. "That's even better than shirts versus skins."

So it was Dougie and me against Mike and Deuce.

"Specs versus pecs," said Mike, flexing his nonexistent pectoral muscles.

The joking stopped when the game started. Mike and Deuce were both good players, and our team was tough, too. Dougie had some really slick moves.

There was no one else there, so we decided to play full court. The game went back and forth for a while. We were up 5–4, but the other team had the ball. Dougie was all over Deuce, slapping at the ball and being a real pest. Deuce had this look on his face like: *Get him off me, man!*

Mike wasn't really ready for the ball, but Deuce fired it anyway. I stepped in front of the pass, and I was off and running. Now I had the ball and clear sailing to the hoop. It was time to see if all my hard work had paid off.

I was all alone by the time I reached the free throw line. I gathered the ball in, took a few steps, and launched myself into the air. As I rose toward the rim, I pulled the ball back and slammed it forward.

Buh-DOING!

At the last second, the very bottom of the ball hit the very top of the rim and the ball shot straight up into the air. So close! I had missed a dunk by a few millimeters! It was close enough that I could've blamed the paint on the rim, if that stuff hadn't peeled off years ago.

Everyone else had given up on the play, so I was still all by myself. I waited for the ball to come down, collected my own rebound, and laid it up and in.

"You were right there!" said Deuce, when he finally arrived to inbound the ball. "Right there!"

"Another inch and you would've had it," said Dougie.

"Not even an inch!" said Mike.

It was the closest I'd ever come to dunking, but I still needed a little more. Even though I was having a great time and Team Specs was up 6–4, I knew I'd have those sweaty old backpacks on again tomorrow.

I still had a few more days to go before the tournament. I hoped it would be enough.

CHAPTER 15

*I*t wasn't hard to convince Dad to drop me off extra early on Saturday. That let him get a head start on all the grass that had grown after the rainstorm — and it was a quicker trip anyway now that his truck was all tuned up.

"Is this it?" said Dad, slowing down in front of a big high school.

I double-checked the name I'd written down. The practices had been on a blazing hot court, but the game was being held in an air-conditioned high school gym.

"Yep," I said. "Gym is supposed to be out back."

"Big one," said Dad as he turned off the main road and wound his way slowly to the back parking lot.

"Look over there," I said as we pulled to a stop. Just outside the doors to the gym, a man with a microphone was talking to a guy holding a big TV camera. A news van from the local station was parked off to the side.

"That's the sports guy from the local news," said Dad.

"Man, this is gonna be big," I said.

The whole trip over, excitement and nervousness had been battling it out inside me. My nerves launched a powerful offensive as I climbed down out of Dad's truck. I think he could tell, because he said: "Good luck today, STAT. You'll do great. I'll try to swing by for some of the game, and you know Junior will be here."

I adjusted my goggles and forced a smile, so he'd know I was ready. Then I headed through the doors. The gym was huge, with row after row of bleachers. They were still mostly empty, but the whole place echoed with the sound of basketballs. A solid hour before we were supposed to be there, the court was already half full. Right in the center, I saw the familiar figure of Coach Dunn. Volunteers were moving around the edge of the court, setting up tables and decorations.

Coach had his head on a swivel and he saw me

coming before anyone else. He walked straight toward me and met me at the edge of the court. He was wearing an official-looking red shirt, with a name tag hanging around his neck alongside a whistle. I thought I might be in trouble.

"How's the eye?" he said.

That's when I remembered: The last time he'd seen me was when he took me to the hospital.

"Good," I told him. "Doesn't hurt at all anymore, and I can see fine. Just supposed to wear these." I reached up and tapped my goggles.

"Glad to hear it," he said. "You had me worried there."

I could hear the relief in his voice.

"I'm ready to play, Coach," I said. I wondered if he could hear the relief in my voice, too.

"Well, hustle over," he said. "Enough of you are here early that we can sneak in a quick practice."

I headed straight for the court. There were six other kids there, and every single one of them was looking at me. I'd gotten so used to my goggles that it took me a while to realize that that's what they were staring at.

"You got something on your face, Pee-wee," I heard. The voice and the comment were both low. The last time I'd seen Monster, he'd just poked me in the eye and sent me to the hospital. I guess he wasn't big on apologies.

"Shut up, man," said Jammer. "Those look cool."

"Looks like a windshield," said Monster, not shutting up. "Do bugs splatter on 'em during fast breaks?"

A few of the other kids laughed, but they stopped when Khalid asked: "How's the eye?"

"Feels good," I said.

"Cool," said Khalid.

"Take some shots," said Jammer. "I'll rebound for you."

Daniel, the other point guard, bounced a ball my way. I spent a few minutes warming up and finding the range on my jump shot.

Coach was waiting for another guy to show up so he could divide us into fours. He was probably waiting for another big, too, so Monster could pick on someone close to his own size. The next guy who showed up was

Tevin. He'd been the center on my team at practice, so that killed two birds with one large stone.

Monster gave him a vicious look, but Tevin ignored him. He came over to me and asked me how I was doing, and if I was cleared to play.

"Yeah," I said, "definitely."

"Those things bother you?" he said, nodding toward my goggles.

"Nah," I said. "Half the time I forget I have them on."

"Cool," he said. "Thinking about getting myself a pair. I have to battle some real jerks down low, you know?"

We both looked over at Monster. "Oh, I know," I said.

Coach blew the whistle and started dividing us up.

"We're going to run with the same teams as the real game," he said. "Once everyone is here, we'll have seven a side. That's a short bench and it's a full game. Don't get crazy, especially now. We're just going to warm up, get the juices flowing."

It was called a tournament, but it was really an exhibition. It was the best kids in the area divided up into two teams and going at it for forty minutes. But most of these kids were in seventh and eighth grade, almost ready for big-time high school hoops. That's why the crowd was already filing in. That's why the light on top of the TV camera courtside flashed on as soon as we started dividing up.

Overall, I felt really good about my team. Khalid was on the other squad, but Daniel was good, too. And Tevin was on my team again, instead of Monster. Most importantly, Jammer was on my side. We bumped fists as Coach called his name.

"We're going to rock this," he said.

"No doubt."

"Okay, ten minutes or so," said Coach. "Nice and easy."

Jammer won the opening tip, and we were off and running. Nice and easy went out the window with the first hard pick. Everyone was ready for today and on their game. Man, these guys were fast — and good! No disrespect to Team Specs or anything, but these guys were on a different level. For the first few possessions, I mostly just tried to keep up.

Once both teams had scored a few times, I started feeling better. I was matched up with a long, lean dude named Delmon. Wayne, the guy I'd matched up with at the first practice, had turned his ankle the week before. It must have been pretty bad, because he was still out and people were still talking about it. I felt bad for him, but now I had to size up this new guy.

I was staying with Delmon without too much trouble, but I was pretty sure he wasn't showing me everything he had. That's okay, I wasn't showing him everything I had, either. This was just a "nice and easy" mini-practice, after all. And there was a good chance we'd end up guarding each other in the real game.

Pretty soon a couple more kids showed up, and we were running five on five. One of the assistant coaches started barking out plays for the other team. Then the other one showed up and started running the show for ours. Coach Dunn mostly played ref and kept things from getting too rough.

By the time the last kids showed up, they just had to take a seat and watch. Our ten minutes had turned to twenty, and there wasn't much point in subbing in now. Daniel drove the lane and set me up with a no-look pass. I did my part, knocking down a ten-footer. A minute later, Delmon launched a fade-away jumper. He created a lot of space quickly, and all I could do was wave at it and hope he missed. He didn't.

Delmon was starting to dial it up as the practice went on. He was an inch or two taller than me with long arms. I was getting a little worried that his length was going to be a problem for me in the game. He got off a floater in the lane on his team's next possession. I turned around to try to box him out, but he kind of muscled his way in beside me. We both watched the ball clank off the front of the rim. Our legs coiled underneath us, and we launched ourselves up toward the rim.

We were so close together that I saw four hands headed up toward the ball. But then something amazing happened. Two of those hands stopped and two of them — mine! — kept going. I grabbed the ball just below the rim and ripped down the rebound.

I passed the ball out to Daniel and sprinted up court with a smile on my face. I'd never jumped that high for a rebound before. Delmon was taller than me, with longer arms, but I'd out-jumped him.

A minute later, Coach blew his whistle and called us

in. He gave us some last-minute instructions, and some-where behind us an air horn sounded. Game on. By the time he sent us over to our benches, the bleachers were full, and I was one hundred percent ready to play.

Unfortunately, it wasn't up to me.

CHAPTER 16

I started the game on the bench. I guess I shouldn't have been too surprised. I was the youngest player on either team, and I'd missed those practices. I was disappointed, but when I looked down my team's bench, I didn't have to look far. There was just one other player, a guy named Harris. After him came a few feet of empty bench and Assistant Coach Perez, who was in charge of our half of things. With a bench that short, it wouldn't be too long before I got my shot.

Out on the court, the game was just getting started. Coach Dunn was acting as referee and head cheerleader. Delmon set a moving screen that just about floored

Daniel. That gave Khalid all the space he needed to rocket to the hoop for a layup. The crowd cheered. Instead of blowing his whistle for the foul, Coach shouted, "There you go!"

On the next possession, Daniel got bumped a little on the way to the hoop for his own layup. It wasn't much contact, but Coach blew his whistle. It was part make-up call and part crowd-pleaser. Everyone loved an and-one. Right then, I knew that Coach wanted two things today: a good game and a fair one — in that order!

I looked over to see if Coach Perez had noticed. A little smile flashed across his face, telling me he had. He sat back and looked down the bench at his two reserves. I straightened out my legs in front of me and reached down and touched my toes. I wanted him to know that I was warmed up and ready to go in at any moment. He smiled again: He'd seen it all before.

I leaned back and looked up into the stands. This was the biggest gym I'd ever been in, and it was full. It took me a while to find Junior — even though he wasn't exactly a small guy. Once I did, I saw Mike and Deuce right next to him. I glanced over at Coach Perez. Once I was sure he wasn't looking, I gave them all a quick wave.

Junior was watching the game, but Mike saw me and waved back. Then he nudged Deuce, who did the same. I waved one more time, so I wouldn't leave Deuce hanging.

"Head in the game," I heard from the end of the bench.

I groaned. Two waves was one wave too many. "Yes, Coach," I said.

I felt a little bad about getting caught, but more than that I felt embarrassed to be on the bench. My brother and friends had come to watch me play, and here I was riding the pine. Then I remembered all those days Mike and Deuce had spent helping me get ready, and I felt even worse. All I could do was lean forward and get my "head in the game."

The good news: Coach made his first sub right after that. The bad news: It was Harris. The other team had taken Monster out for a breather, and our coach took the opportunity to give Tevin a quick rest, too. Those two had been battling like a pair of angry rhinos in the paint.

Tevin sat down next to me. He was already sweaty five minutes in, and the bench creaked under his weight.

"You're doing great out there," I said.

"Thanks, that guy's a beast," he said, nodding over toward Monster on the other bench.

"You are too," I said. "It's like two beasts in a box when you guys go for a rebound."

Tevin laughed. "Beasts in a box," he said. "I like that."

A shadow fell over us while we were talking. We looked up and saw the TV cameraman standing over us. The camera was on his shoulder and pointed down at Tevin. I guess they wanted footage of a real live (real sweaty) beast. Tevin did his part, flashing them a smile and a peace sign.

"Think this is live?" I asked, once the camera guy moved on.

"Nah, they're just going to chop it up into a little piece for the news," he said. "They'll show some high-lights and maybe interview a few of the players."

I nodded, trying to act like it wouldn't be my first

time on TV. Not that I'd be in any highlights if our coach didn't put me in. A minute later, I got my chance. Harris made a turnover under our own basket, leading to two quick points for the other team. I looked up at the scoreboard: They were ahead 20–17.

Coach Perez shot to his feet and put his hands on both sides of his mouth. "No, no, no!" he shouted. "We can't give them cheap buckets — squeeze that thing!" Then he turned to me. "Go get him!" he said.

He meant to sub in for Harris at the next whistle, and he didn't have to tell me twice. I was up off the bench and headed for the scorer's table in an eyeblink. Finally!

The ball flew out of bounds on the far side, and the whistle blew. I shot a quick look back at Junior, Mike, and Deuce and gave them a quick nod. Then I sprinted out onto the court, readjusting my goggles one last time as I went.

I let Harris know he was out and let Daniel know I was in. Jammer saw me and we bumped forearms. A few possessions went by, and the teams traded buckets.

Khalid scored on a floater for them, and Braylon scored on a jumper for us.

Braylon was the guy who'd guarded Jammer at the first practice. He had a nice midrange game, and I was glad he was on our team this time.

"Nice shot, Braylon!" I called.

He gave me that little pistol-point with his index finger as we all hustled back on defense. I was on Delmon again, and I had to work hard to stay with him. He was pretty fast and liked to weave in and out of traffic. I guess I shouldn't have been surprised at what happened next.

Delmon had the ball and was going at top speed up near the free throw line. I was sprinting to stay with him. At one point, I was almost close enough to take a swipe at the ball. I took a swipe at it anyway. I saw my fingers come up a few inches short, and then everything went dark.

The next thing I saw: stars. I was sitting down on the court and checking to see if I still had all my parts. I moved my feet and hands, so they were still there. I looked up, so my neck still worked. And there was Monster.

TWEEEEET!

Coach blew his whistle for the moving screen. It felt more like a pick play in football. Jammer and Braylon reached down and helped me up. I reached up to my face. My nose stung a little where the goggles had been smashed back into it, but I was glad they were in one piece.

"Think I got goggle prints on my chest," said Monster as he walked away. A few of his teammates laughed.

We got the ball back for the offensive foul, and Daniel told me to be ready. I inbounded the ball to him and took off down the court.

I think Delmon was a little afraid my team was going to knock him down or run him into Tevin as payback. He was playing a little off me and looking around the whole time. Daniel noticed. He waited until Delmon was a few feet away, then fired a chest-high, two-handed pass right to me.

Delmon tried to make up the ground by leaping at me. I shaded off to the side and got the shot off right before he landed on me. The shot banked off the backboard and in as Delmon crashed down on me. I didn't mind ending up on the ground again. I knew my teammates would help me up — and I knew I'd be going to the line. Coach blew his whistle: Everyone loved an and-one.

I drained the free throw to complete the three-point play. The score was tied at 22 all, and I was on the board. I settled into the flow of the game after that. There were a few times, waiting for the play to start or the ball to be inbounded, when I noticed what was going on around us. I saw the crowd and the light on top of the TV camera and all that. I admit it was a little weird to be out there in front of so many strangers with the goggles on. But most of the time, I was too busy to give it a second thought.

The game stayed tight for the rest of the half, and the pace stayed fast. I scored twice — once inside and once outside — and Delmon scored once. Jammer was doing most of the damage for our team. I got an assist on an above-the-rim alley-oop pass to him.

"I didn't know he could go *that* high," said Daniel.

"I've played with him before," I said with a shrug.

A little later, Daniel fed him with a perfect alley-oop of his own. After Jammer powered it home, Daniel pointed one finger at him and one at me. I thought that was pretty cool.

All those dunks made me want to get in on the action. I kept looking for a chance to try one of my own. But I still needed a clear path to the hoop — some runway for my takeoff — and those opportunities didn't exactly grow on trees. As tight as the game was, it seemed more important to play good D and smart offense.

Khalid was getting the job done for the other team. He was using his speed and Monster's size to create mismatches. Toward the end of the half, I found myself in a tangle of bodies down low. We switched and switched again, trying to keep everyone covered.

Suddenly, I was on Monster, and Khalid had the ball. Khalid was my friend, but I knew that he wouldn't hesitate to take advantage of the size mismatch. I heard Coach Perez shouting from the bench: "Front him! Front him!"

I used every bit of speed I had to slip out from behind Monster. Then I lunged forward and shot my hand out as far as it would go.

BAPPP!

I got a piece of the ball. It was just enough to deflect the pass and keep it out of Monster's hands. The clock ran out as everyone was scrambling for the loose ball. I looked up at the scoreboard. It was a flat-footed tie: 48–48.

CHAPTER 17

Dad arrived at halftime. I took a quick look up into the stands while our coach was telling us about some changes we needed to make on defense. I saw Junior scooching over and Dad settling in between him and my friends. I looked up a little later and saw Junior giving him a quick recap. He was reaching his hand all the way out in front of him to show Dad how I'd deflected the pass away from Monster.

Coach Perez started talking about some offensive plays and then looked over at me. I sat up a little straighter. "Amar'e, I want to get you a little more involved in the scoring," he said. *Sounds good to me!* I thought. "I think you can take your guy. And a few buckets from you will make it harder for them to keep double-teaming Jammer."

I nodded. Jammer extended his hand and we fist-bumped. I was happy that I wouldn't be starting this half on the bench. Coach Perez seemed to have his rotation set now, and I was a big part of it.

We all took a few last drinks of water and then headed back onto the court. Coach Dunn was standing in the center with his whistle in his mouth and a big smile stretching out on either side of it. He wanted a good game, and he was getting one.

The second half stayed tight, and I was definitely getting my hands on the ball more now. Almost every time we were on offense, it came my way. Sometimes it was just to pass it around the outside or something like that. But a few times, I got it down low or Daniel hit me with a pass as I was cutting to the hoop. Then I could do some work!

I was a little faster than Delmon: not enough to blow by him, but enough to get my shot off. I burned him with a jumper for my first hoop of the half. A few minutes later, when he was looking for the jumper, I slipped past him with an up-and-under move.

"Lucky," said Delmon. The way he spat out the word, I knew he was mad. I wasn't surprised when he tried to run me into another Monster-size pick on the other end. I just ducked under it and picked him up on the other side.

"I'm gonna eat those goggles," said Monster as I passed.

Eat my goggles? That didn't even make any sense. But I knew one thing: If the other team is mad at you, you're doing something right. I just shook my head and stayed on Delmon until he had to give up the ball.

And our coach was right, too. Just a few quick hoops from me caused all kinds of confusion for the other team's D. The next time down the court, I got good position near the rim. I put my hands up for the ball. Monster saw it and took a few steps over toward me, to help out Delmon or possibly to eat my goggles.

Either way, it opened up the lane. Jammer was more than happy to fill it with a huge, one-handed dunk that brought the whole crowd to its feet. It also put us up by five, our largest lead of the game.

The good news didn't even last long enough for the crowd to sit back down. Monster had tried to jump back into the play. He was way too late, but he kept going anyway. He slid under the rim just as Jammer was letting go of it and dropping back down to the court.

Jammer's right leg hit Monster's left shoulder, and he took a nasty spill down onto the court. At the last second, he put his right hand down to break his fall. He hit hard and rolled over. His face was twisted in pain and he was holding his wrist.

Our entire team headed straight there. Half of us wanted to make sure Jammer was okay, and half of us wanted to make sure Monster wouldn't be. Or, I take that back. All of us wanted to do both, it was just a question of which to do first. Coach Dunn blew his whistle and kept blowing it: *TWEEEEEEEEEEEEEEEEEEET!*

He stepped in front of Monster like he was boxing him out for a rebound. Really he was trying to keep us all away from him.

"That was a cheap shot!" shouted Daniel.

Other people said things that were a lot worse.

"It was an accident!" said Monster. And maybe it had been, but I'd noticed that people seemed to have an awful lot of "accidents" around that guy.

"It was a boneheaded move either way, Maurice," said Coach Dunn. I guess that was Monster's real name. "Anything else from you and you're gone!"

Monster rolled his eyes, but he knew enough not to argue. I couldn't believe Coach wasn't kicking him out of the game. I slipped past Coach and knelt down next to Jammer. "You okay, man?" I said.

"No," he said through gritted teeth. "I just got hit by a big, ugly truck."

I laughed. The fact that he was joking at all meant it probably wasn't too bad.

"Wrist's not broken?" I said.

"Nah, I don't think so," he said. "Smacked it pretty good, though."

Someone brought an ice pack in from the sidelines, and a few of us helped Jammer to his feet. The crowd stopped booing Monster and started clapping for Jammer.

Our whole team was still really mad when the game

started up again. We got two free throws, and Braylon drained them both to put our team up by seven. Then Khalid led his team up court at top speed as our squad hustled back on defense. The only person who didn't run full-out was Monster, who barely jogged. I think he was mad his team hadn't backed him up.

Up ahead, Daniel deflected a pass to Harris, who'd come in for Jammer. I saw it the whole way and broke back toward our basket. I was already at midcourt when my old bench buddy saw me. He pulled the ball back over his shoulder and launched a long pass right to me. I caught it over my shoulder, like a wide receiver, and started dribbling.

There was only one man between me and the basket. Monster suddenly found himself back in the play. I went right at him, and that caught him by surprise. He started backpedaling. He was inside the free throw line now, still giving ground. In another few seconds, I was there, too. I knew what I had to do. I dribbled it once, twice, and then it was time for takeoff!

Monster knew it, too: He planted his feet and put his left arm straight up.

I didn't know if I could throw down my first dunk at all, and I definitely didn't know if I could do it over this beast. But I was definitely going to try: This one was for Jammer!

I took one last step and leapt into the air. An image flashed through my mind: Me jumping up onto that old park bench, the backpacks flapping against me as I landed.

I pulled my arm back above my head, holding the ball as tightly as I could in my hand. Another image: Jammer rolling in pain, Monster standing over him.

My momentum pushed Monster's arm and shoulder aside. I brought the ball forward. And. Threw. It. Down!

I felt the heel of my palm slap the metal of the rim. Out of the corner of my eye — well, of my lens — I saw the orange flash of the ball shoot down past me toward the court. I dropped down after it.

"Yes!" I shouted as my sneakers landed on the court.

I heard cheers rise up all around me, and I turned around in time to see Monster shaking his head. I didn't even have to say it: He'd just been posterized. I pointed over at Jammer, who was already standing and shouting.

He pointed back at me with his left hand, and we both nodded.

After that, I looked up in the stands. I knew right where Dad, Junior, Mike, and Deuce were, but I could only see the top of Dad's head at first. Everyone else was standing, too. But as the people around them sat back down, they kept standing and cheering.

My dunk put us up by nine, and we cruised from there. After the final seconds ran out, I headed over to our bench to check on Jammer and celebrate with the rest of the team.

It didn't take my family and friends long to make their way through the crowd and join the celebration. I got a hug from Dad and high fives from the rest of them. Junior pointed his thumb at Deuce and said: "This guy was telling half the people in our row that he's your 'personal trainer'!"

"Yeah, that sounds about right," I said. "But only half of 'em?"

A sly grin crept onto Deuce's face. "Yeah, mostly the girls," he said.

We all got a good laugh out of that. Then Mike chimed in: "And I don't remember him mentioning me, either: the brains of the operation!"

That was even funnier, but as I shook my head at their goofy jokes, I knew it was true. I couldn't have done it without them. I didn't just mean the dunk, either. That was the least of it. I thought back: The first tournament I'd ever played in, I'd played with them. I thought about all the days we'd played hoops until the sun went down.

Then I looked over at Dad and Junior, and thought about how much I owed them, too. I mean, where do I even start that list?

"Hey, STAT," I heard.

"Yeah, Dad?"

"Looks like Coach wants you for something."

I turned around. Coach was standing with Tevin and Jammer and waving me over. I looked back at my crew. There was still something I wanted to say to them, but Junior shooed me away. "Well, go on," he said. "Don't keep the man waiting."

I headed over. "Yeah, Coach?"

"Someone wants to talk to you three," he said, a big smile on his face. He pointed out onto the court — straight toward the TV camera! The guy with the microphone was standing next to it, straightening his sports jacket and waiting for us.

"Nice," said Tevin as we headed over.

The sportscaster introduced himself and shook our hands. He shook Tevin's first and told him, "Good game!" Then he shook Jammer's left hand and asked him how his right was feeling. He shook my hand and said, "Sweet dunk!" Then he looked at my goggles and asked, "You want to take those off before the interview?"

"Nah," I said. "I'm good."

"Well," he said. "Let's start with you, then." The light on top of the TV camera blinked on, and the sportscaster asked his first question. "Your dunk over a much bigger player was the highlight of the game. Is there anything you'd like to say about it?"

I wasn't sure if I was supposed to look at him or the camera. I decided to look at him because he was the one asking the question. "It was my first dunk, and it was for my friend Jammer here," I said.

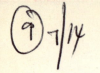

He nodded. He seemed happy with that. "Anything else?" he said.

And there was something else: "Just that I'd like to thank my dad; my brother, Junior; and my boys Mike and Deuce."

It was what I'd been meaning to say the whole time.

12/19-14